OllietheStomper

Olivier Dunrea

WALKER BOOKS
AND SUBSIDIARIES
LONDON · BOSTON · SYDNEY · AUCKLAND

For Mack

First published in Great Britain 2004 by Walker Books Ltd
87 Vauxhall Walk, London SE11 5HJ

This edition published 2006

2 4 6 8 10 9 7 5 3 1

© 2003 Olivier Dunrea
Published by arrangement with Houghton Mifflin Company

This book has been typeset in Shannon

Printed in China

British Library Cataloguing in Publication Data:
a catalogue record for this book is available from the British Library

ISBN-13: 978-1-4063-0121-2
ISBN-10: 1-4063-0121-3

www.walkerbooks.co.uk

This is Ollie.

This is Gossie. This is Gertie.

They are goslings.

Gossie wears bright red boots.

Gertie wears bright blue boots.

Ollie wants boots.

Gossie and Gertie tromp in the straw.

Ollie stomps after them.

Gossie and Gertie romp in the rain.

Ollie stomps after them.

Gossie and Gertie jump over a puddle.

Ollie stomps after them.

Gossie and Gertie march to the pond.

Ollie stomps after them.

Gossie and Gertie hide in the pumpkins.

"*I want boots!*" Ollie shouts.

Gossie and Gertie stomp to Ollie.

Gossie gives Ollie a red boot.

Gertie gives Ollie a blue boot.

Ollie hops to the barn.

Gossie and Gertie follow.

Ollie stomps to the pigsty.

Gossie and Gertie follow.

Ollie stares at his boots.

"*These boots are too hot!*" Ollie shouts.

Ollie kicks off his boots.

Gossie kicks off her boot.
Gertie kicks off her boot.

"Let's go swimming!" Ollie shouts.
And they do.